I0614227

Better Book Reports

Aligned to Common Core

—— Grades 7 to 8 ——

Written by Eleanor M. Summers

This resource contains six sections: **Vocabulary Development, Identifying Important Information, Character Analysis, Summarizing and Sequencing Events, Reasoning and Critical Thinking,** and **Creativity and Design.** Each section begins with a Teacher's Notes page that will provide suggestions to help you to introduce the sections and to obtain the best results from your students. Students in the Intermediate Division have more sophisticated reading skills and require purposeful and challenging activities that will promote successful and enjoyable reading experiences.

Book reports allow the young readers to share their thoughts about the stories they have heard or have read themselves. As well, students need the opportunity to demonstrate their understanding of the materials.

Eleanor Summers is a retired elementary teacher who continues to be involved in various levels of education. Her goal is to write creative and practical resources for teachers to use in their literacy programs.

Published in Canada by:
On The Mark Press
15 Dairy Avenue, Napanee, Ontario, K7R 1M4
www.onthemarkpress.com

OTM18131   ISBN: 9781770788565
© On The Mark Press

MEETING THE COMMON CORE STATE STANDARDS

Each lesson and student activity worksheet meets one or more of the following standards from the Common Core State Standards Initiative for English Language Arts.

I. LITERATURE AND INFORMATIONAL TEXTS		
Key Ideas and Details		
CCSS#	**Standard**	**Page Number**
RL.7/8.2 RI.7/8.2	Identify the theme of the story Summarize the text	43, 46, 47, 59, 60
Craft and Structure		
CCSS#	**Standard**	**Page Number**
RL.7/8.5	Identify differences in genres: formats and structures	11, 12, 14
Range of Reading and Level of Text Complexity		
CCSS#	**Standard**	**Page Number**
RL.7/8.10	Read and comprehend grade-level literature	12, 14, 17, 18, 19, 20, 22, 23, 27, 29, 30, 33, 34, 35, 37, 38, 39, 41, 42, 43, 44, 45, 46, 47, 49, 50, 51, 52, 53, 54, 55, 57, 58, 59, 60, 61, 62, 63
RI.3/4.7	Read and comprehend grade-level informational texts	12, 14, 21, 22, 25, 26, 28, 38, 44, 45, 49, 51, 52, 53, 55, 59, 60, 62, 63
II. LANGUAGE		
Conventions of Standard English		
CCSS#	**Standard**	**Page Number**
L.7.1b	Use a variety of sentences to convey ideas	18
Vocabulary Acquisition and Use		
CCSS#	**Standard**	**Page Number**
L.7/8.4a	Use context clues to determine word meaning	10
L.7/8.4c	Use reference materials: dictionary, glossary, thesaurus	11, 21, 26
L.7/8.5	Explain the meaning of figurative language and word relationships	21, 23
L.7/8.5b	Use word relationships to explain their meanings	20

OTM18131   ISBN: 9781770788565
© On The Mark Press

III. WRITING

Text Types and Purposes

CCSS#	Standard	Page Number
W.7/8.1	Support claims with clear reasons and evidence	39, 46, 50, 51, 52, 55
W.7/8.2	Write an informative or explanatory text	28, 53, 54
W.7/8.2a	Write a report using proper text, graphics and illustrations	25, 30, 31, 35, 38, 41, 44, 45, 47, 57, 58, 59, 61, 62
W.7/8.2c	Use transitional words, phrases and clauses	17
W.7/8.2d	Use precise language to inform or explain	22, 27
W.7/8.3	Write narratives to develop real or imagined characters or events. Compare and contrast characters and events	29, 33, 34, 37, 49

Production and Distribution of Writing

CCSS#	Standard	Page Number
W.7/8.4	Write for a purpose and a specific audience	36, 42

IV. SPEAKING AND LISTENING

Comprehension and Collaboration

CCSS#	Standard	Page Number
SL.7/8.1	Evaluate personal performance	5

Presentation of Knowledge and Ideas

CCSS#	Standard	Page Number
SL.7/8.4	Present and sequence facts and ideas clearly	6
SL.7/8.5	Clarify information using multimedia, audio or visual displays	57, 60, 61, 63

Learning Expectations

	Vocabulary Development	Identifying Important Information	Character Analysis	Summarizing & Sequencing Events	Reasoning & Critical Thinking	Creativity & Design
Oral Communication						
Listen and respond orally to stories and poems.	•	•	•	•	•	•
Respond to text by describing personal experiences and retelling familiar stories, using basic story structure: beginning, middle, end.		•	•	•	•	•
Retell a story by adapting it for presentation in another way.	•	•	•	•	•	•
Rephrase information to clarify and expand ideas.	•	•			•	•
Vocabulary Development						
Identify parts of speech: nouns, verbs, modifiers.	•	•	•	•	•	
Use connecting phrase and clauses to retell a story.	•	•			•	•
Use a variety of sentence types and explain their use.	•					
Identify figurative language: simile, metaphor, imagery, personification.	•	•	•	•	•	
Paraphrase a section to clarify meaning.	•	•		•	•	
Use a dictionary and thesaurus to expand vocabulary.	•	•			•	
Reading Skills						
Identify and describe the character traits of primary and secondary characters.		•	•	•	•	•
Identify and describe story elements. Explain relationship to each other.		•	•	•	•	•
Summarize story elements, giving evidence to support answers.		•	•	•	•	•
Recall information about the characters, the action, and the ending.		•	•	•	•	•
Predict events and characters' actions and reactions		•	•	•	•	•
Reasoning & Critical Thinking						
Become familiar with a variety of genres.	•	•	•	•	•	•
Determine if a story is real or make believe: fiction or non-fiction, using evidence from the story.		•	•	•	•	
Restate information in a non-fiction text.		•		•	•	•
Use knowledge of the story to predict what may happen next: revise or confirm predictions.		•	•	•	•	
Identify and describe similarities and differences.		•	•		•	•
Draw conclusions and begin to make inferences.		•	•	•	•	
Identify the problem and the solution in a story.		•	•	•	•	
Retell a story ending; make up an alternate ending or a sequel .			•	•	•	
Identify the point of view of the author or a character.		•	•	•	•	
Identify literary techniques: foreshadowing, mood, theme.		•	•	•	•	
Make connections between the story, personal experiences, and real world.		•	•	•	•	
Develop an opinion, judge a story, and make a recommendation to other readers.			•		•	•
Develop an appreciation for good literature and outstanding authors and illustrators.		•			•	•
Creativity & Design						
Express feelings and emotions in a visual art form.		•	•	•	•	•
Demonstrate an understanding of the story through music, drama or visual arts.		•	•	•	•	
Create a visual product or media text using ideas from the story.		•	•	•	•	•

OTM18131   ISBN: 9781770788565
© On The Mark Press

TABLE OF CONTENTS

Teacher Assessment Rubric

Student's Name: _____   Date: _____

Put a check mark in the box that indicates the student's level of achievement.

Level 1 – requires assistance, inconsistent effort, shows limited understanding of concepts
Level 2 – requires minimal assistance, shows limited understanding of concepts
Level 3 – independent, consistent effort, shows general understanding of concepts
Level 4 – independent, consistent effort, shows thorough understanding of concepts

Success Criteria	Level 1	Level 2	Level 3	Level 4
Oral Communication				
Retells familiar stories making personal connections				
Rephrases information to clarify and expand ideas				
Vocabulary Development				
Understands the text at word level				
Recognizes and understands figurative and expressive language				
Uses dictionary and thesaurus to expand vocabulary				
Identifying Important Information				
Identifies main idea and gives supporting details				
Evaluates story elements and problem resolution				
Draws conclusions; forms personal interpretation of story				
Character Analysis				
Identifies and describes main and other characters				
Compares characters and their traits				
Evaluates roles of characters				
Summarizing & Sequencing Events				
Retells a story in proper sequence; recalls details				
Identifies and describes some story elements				
Reasoning & Critical Thinking				
Makes predictions, inferences, and conclusions				
Distinguishes between fact and fiction				
Develops opinion; expresses personal point of view				
Identifies the problem and solution in a story				
Analyzes and evaluates story elements				
Creativity & Design				
Expresses feelings and emotions in a visual form				
Demonstrates an understanding of the story through music, drama, and visual arts.				
Creates a media text form.				

OTM18131   ISBN: 9781770788565
© On The Mark Press

Student Self Assessment Rubric

Name:_____

Put a check mark in the box that best describes your performance. Then add up your points (pts) to find your total score.

Expectations	Always (4 pts)	Often (3 pts)	Some-times (2 pts)	Seldom (1 pt)	My Points
I remained focused and on task.					
I asked for explanations and assistance when I needed it.					
I was prepared and organized.					
I checked meanings of difficult words and ideas.					
I used my text to support my ideas.					
I rechecked the information so I could rethink my answers.					
I edited and proofread my work.					
I connected the material to my own life and to the real world.					
I know what I do well.					
I know what I need to improve.					
				Total	

The most valuable thing I learned was _____

_____

Student – Teacher Conference Form

Student's Name: _____   Date: _____

Title of book: _____

Retelling Skills

Skill	yes	no
Identifies the setting: time and place		
Names the primary and secondary characters		
States the main character's problem		
Explains the character's actions		
Uses accurate vocabulary in the retelling		

Reasoning Skills

Skill	yes	no
Identifies main idea and provides supporting details Comments:		
Retells the plot in correct sequence Comments:		
Makes predictions, draws conclusions and makes inferences Comments:		
Makes personal connections to the text Comments:		

Additional Comments: _____

_____

_____

Present descriptions, ideas and details in a clear manner   OTM18131   ISBN: 9781770788565
© On The Mark Press

INTRODUCTION & TEACHER SUGGESTIONS

OVERALL EXPECTATIONS

Students in the Intermediate Division have more sophisticated reading skills and require purposeful and challenging activities that will promote successful and enjoyable reading experiences. These activities should address both oral and written aspects of performance.

Oral Communication

- Listen and react to stories and recount personal experiences.
- Communicate thoughts and feelings using age appropriate strategies.
- Express clear responses to written materials by relating to their own knowledge and experiences.

Reading Skills

- Read a variety of written materials: novels, poetry, non-fiction books.
- Read independently using age appropriate strategies.
- Independently select own reading materials.
- Choose materials by a variety of authors and form an opinion about that author.
- Understand the vocabulary and language structures for this grade level.
- Use the conventions of written language (title, punctuation, pictures) to assist in understanding the text.

Reading and understanding the text is the initial step for these activities. With teacher guidance and modeling, students can apply their understanding to produce their own interpretation of what they have read.

INTRODUCTION

As teachers of Intermediate level students, we want to encourage our students to expand their reading repertoire and to showcase their understanding in ways that appeal to them. We need valid methods for monitoring what they are reading and what impressions have been formed. Book reports allow the young readers to share their thoughts about the stories they have heard or have read themselves. Book reports should include those relating to personal experiences and background to their newly acquired information. Book report activities can involve oral presentations, written reports, dramatic, musical and visual arts experiences.

Teachers can use book report activities to:

- Extend the young readers' experiences by encouraging them to read different genres.
- Offer a wide variety of activities.
- Assess student understanding and ability to connect to prior learning.
- Foster independent work habits by giving guided choices.

SELECTING & ORGANIZING THE CLASSROOM MATERIALS & ACTIVITIES

Ideally, we want to have our students exposed to a greater variety of suitable reading materials and to ensure that they are exploring new materials. We need to provide access to appropriate materials and to encourage the students to make good choices: interesting topics, appropriate level of difficulty, new forms of reading.

A classroom should have its own large supply of reading materials. Most teachers combine their own collections with resources from the school or public library. Select a variety of materials that meet these criteria:

- quality material with well-written text
- content that can be linked to the curriculum as much as possible
- appealing, colorful illustrations
- interesting and challenging text
- pattern and predictable plot
- age appropriate subject matter
- variety of text from recognized authors and illustrators

Suggested Reading Materials for Intermediate Students

For book report activities, Grade 7 and 8 students should read literature in these areas:

- novels
- poetry
- folk and fairy tales, legends, myths
- graphic novels
- non-fiction books: science, social studies, health, cookbooks
- biographies, autobiographies, memoirs
- historical fiction, science fiction, adventure, mystery
- maps, graphs
- comic books, magazines, joke books

Try to provide a balance of fiction and non-fiction, old favorites and new titles, and a variety of authors and illustrators.

SETTING UP THE CLASSROOM LIBRARY

Although Intermediate students can acquire reading materials from a variety of sources, you still may wish to select an area of your classroom where you can set up your classroom reading materials on a permanent basis. Your students will like and use a system that is easy for them. Display some posters or pictures that will draw attention to your library corner. If space permits, supply a mat or big cushions for sitting.

Consider using durable plastic baskets or bins for book storage or these reasons:

- categories (labels on baskets) can be changed
- books are easy for students to put back into the correct place
- books with attractive covers facing out are easy for students to browse
- books are already sorted and are easy to move if necessary.

Suggested Categories for Book Basket Labels

- Adventure and Mystery
- Favorite Author, Favorite Series
- New Books
- Non-fiction Books
- Poetry
- Class Favorites: single books or series
- Fairy Tales, legends
- Biographies
- Graphic novels

ORGANIZING BOOK REPORT ACTIVITIES

There are two areas of organizing and storage for Book Report activities.

1. **Book Report Forms and Materials:** Once your students are able to work independently, you will need a system where they have access to worksheets and materials. Worksheets may be kept in labelled folders in hanging files boxes, in baskets or bins. Students may have free choice or follow your direction in which activity to choose. Ensure that students know your expectations on what needs to be completed and how much time they have to complete their activity.

2. **Completed Student Work:** Have students make a personal reading folder to hold completed work. On the outside of a file folder, tape or glue a copy of the "Personal Reading Record" (see page 15). On the inside of the file folder, glue a copy of "Book Report Activities Tracking Sheet" (see page 16). Ask students to record what materials have been read and

OTM18131 ISBN: 9781770788565
© On The Mark Press

which activities have been completed. Once the students have had an opportunity to share and celebrate their efforts, they could file and store their concrete results. This Book Report folder containing student work will give you the materials to assess student performance and progress.

SHARING STUDENT BOOK REPORTS

An important element for the success of any activity is having the opportunity to share one's efforts with one's peers and with others. Sharing is an opportunity for each student to demonstrate what they have learned and to celebrate their own results. Members of the sharing audience see how others perceive what they have learned and thereby, broaden their own knowledge.

There are a number of ways to share student results. Some suggestions are:

- Oral presentations to one's own class and to other classes.
- Buddy sharing with younger students. Example: a Grade 7-8 student sharing with a Primary or Junior age student.
- Displaying work on a bulletin board that has a prominent place in the school: school foyer, bulletin board outside the gymnasium
- Arrange with the public library to display some student book reports.
- Ask a local newspaper to include a short article or pictures on some work you feel was especially well done or work from some seasonal event.
- Try, as much as possible, to display student book reports on hall bulletin boards instead of classroom bulletin boards.

INTRODUCING BOOK REPORT ACTIVITIES

This resource contains six sections: Vocabulary Development, Identifying Important Information, Character Analysis, Summarizing and Sequencing Events, Reasoning and Critical Thinking, and Creativity and Design. Each section begins with a Teacher's Notes page that will provide suggestions to help you to introduce the sections and to obtain the best results from your students.

- Book reports should be introduced to the whole class after a discussion or mini-lesson. Mini-lessons are found on each Teacher's Notes page. Select books that support the skill focus of the activity (section) you are introducing.
- After the mini-lesson, have the students practice by completing the worksheets to "report" on the chosen books.
- Use the min-lesson format to introduce each section of the Book Report activities.
- Once the activities for each section have been modeled, and students have practiced sufficiently, Book Report activities can be used as an independent student work.

The "Before We Begin" activities section includes activities to try before starting on the Book Report activities. They are:

Library Lingo: Crossword Word Puzzle using terms associated with books and reading

  Page 11 Answers: 4. biography   6. plot
  8. fiction   9. novel   10. title page   14. title
  15. table of contents   17. publisher
  18. illustrator   19. setting   20. autobiography

Genres: Matching Activities:

  Page 12 What Is Genre? (match names of genres to their definitions)
  1. mystery   2. biography   3. fantasy   4. poetry
  5. myth   6. fable   7. science fiction
  8. realistic fiction   9. historical fiction
  10. non-fiction   11. fairy tale   12. reference

  Page 13 Genre Detective (match names of actual examples of literature to genres):
  Answers will vary

Library Lingo

WORD BOX

author
copyright
graphic novel
preview
table of
    contents
autobiography
cover
illustrator
publisher
text
biography

fiction
non-fiction
review
title
chapters
glossary
novel
setting
title page
characters
plot

Match the words in the Word Box to the clues to solve this puzzle.

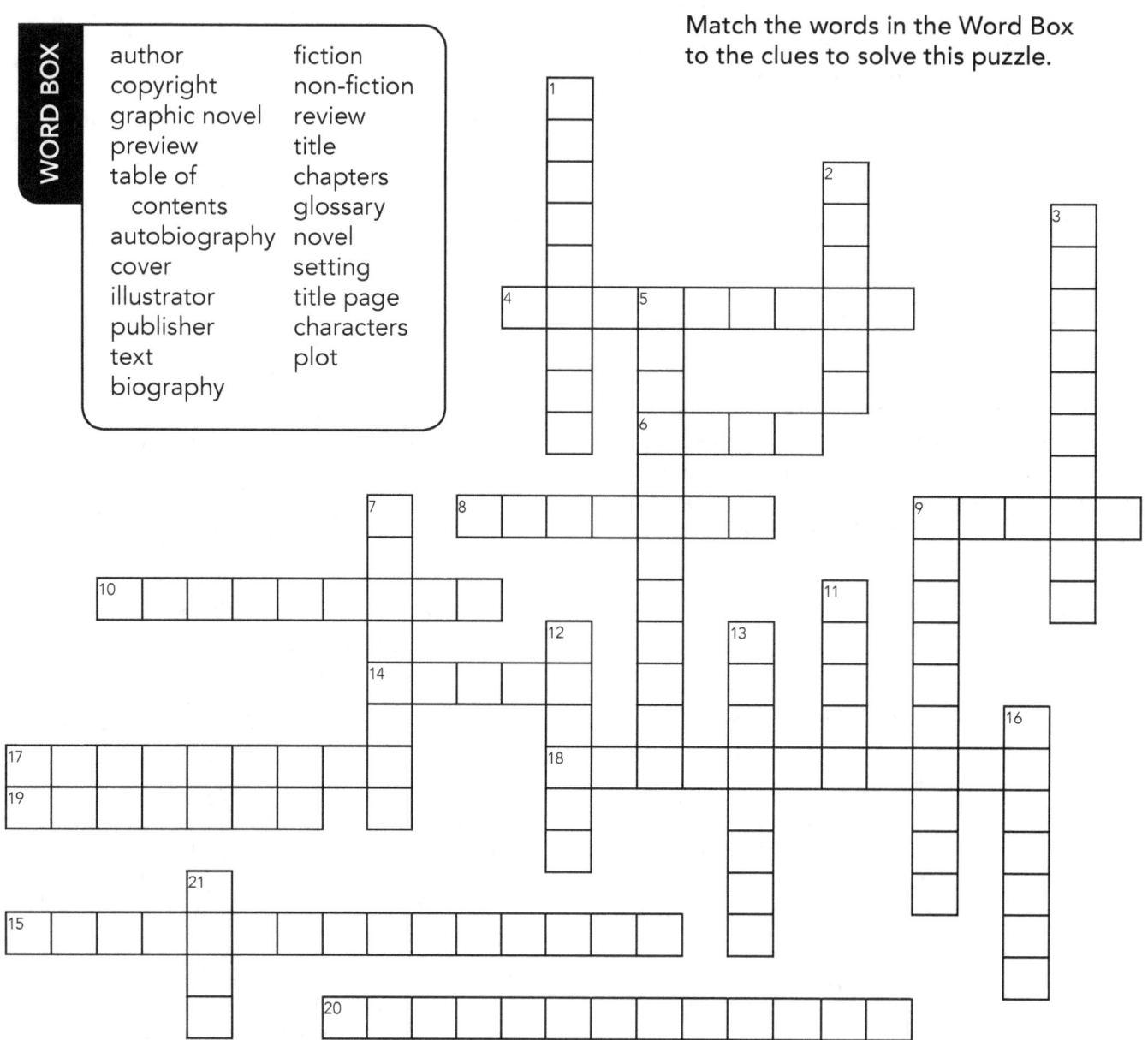

Across:

4. I am a person's life story written by someone else.
6. I am the events that make up a story
8. I am a story that has characters and events that are not real.
9. I am a long story about imaginary people and events
10. I am often the first page in a book. I tell you the name of the story and the author.
14. I tell you the name of the book.
15. I tell what is in the book and what page it is on.
17. I print the pages and make the book.
18. I draw the pictures for a story
19. I tell the time and place where a story takes place.
20. I am a person's life story written by that person

Down:

1. I tell you who owns the material in the book.
2. I write stories and poems.
3. We are the people and animals in the story.
5. I am a novel with many pictures and some text.
7. We are the separate sections of a book.
9. I am a book that has true facts.
11. I can be soft or hard. I am the outside of your book.
12. I tell you about the book and give you my opinion.
13. I am a list of hard words and their meanings. I am usually found at the back of the book.
16. I give you some hints as to what the book will contain.
21. I am the written part of the book.

Use context clues to determine word meanings

OTM18131 ISBN: 9781770788565
© On The Mark Press

What is Genre?

Genre means a category of books that has its own particular style, form and content. Read the names of the genres in the Word Box. Match the name of the genre to the clues. Use a dictionary to help you with the meanings. Check with your librarian.

WORD BOX

Biography	Historical Fiction	Poetry	Fable	Mystery	Realistic Fiction
Fairy Tale	Myths	Reference	Fantasy	Non-Fiction	Science Fiction

Characteristics of book	Name of Genre
• characters are fictional (may be a detective, spy) • there is a problem to be solved • clues are used to find a solution	1.
• a true story about the life of a real person • the author is a different person than the book is written about • we learn how the person affected others	2.
• characters or objects do things that couldn't happen in real life; often there is magic • there is a struggle between good and evil	3.
• it may or may not be written in rhyme • it is often read aloud and touches our feelings	4.
• takes place before people were on earth • tries to explain events or situations in life	5.
• short stories with animal characters that act like humans • there is a lesson or moral to be learned	6.
• contains future ideas such as space travel • characters are fictional • problem is usually solved using science	7.
• characters behave in realistic ways • a problem or conflict needs to be solved • the setting is in modern times	8.
• some characters are real and some are fictional • real events in history are mixed with fictional events • story takes place during a time in history	9.
• contains true facts and information about different subjects • may include charts and maps	10.
• characters are make believe or magic • usually good against evil • often begin with "Once upon a time...."	11.
• provide true facts and information • examples include: dictionary, thesaurus, atlas, almanac, encyclopedia	12.

Genre Detective

Think about what you have learned about different genres. Go on a genre hunt to find titles of books that match each genre. Record the titles on the chart. Write a brief description of what the book contains. (one or two sentences is great!) Ask your teacher or librarian if you need help.

Genre	Title of book	Description
Biography		
Fable		
Fairy Tale		
Fantasy		
Historical Fiction		
Myths		
Mystery		
Non-Fiction		
Poetry		
Realistic Fiction		
Reference		
Science Fiction		

Identify difference in genres
Read grade-level literature and informational text

OTM18131   ISBN: 9781770788565
© On The Mark Press

BOOK REPORT ACTIVITIES

LIST OF WORKSHEETS

Vocabulary Development

1. It's About Time
2. Sentence Sense
3. Similes and Metaphors
4. Stick to the Basics
5. Creating a Glossary
6. In My Words
7. In My Mind I See ...

Identifying Important Information

1. Historically Speaking
2. Reference Round Up
3. Story Tree
4. What's Cooking?
5. The Mystery News
6. Mythology Facts
7. Pictures Matter

Character Analysis

1. Fantastic Characters
2. Out of This World
3. A Room of My Own
4. This Song is Dedicated to...
5. Just Between Us
6. In Honor Of...
7. The Good, The Bad, The In-Betweens

Summarizing & Sequencing Events

1. Cartoon Caper
2. Prose to Script
3. Story Chain
4. It's All About Time
5. Take a Peek
6. And Then What Happened?
7. Get in the Game

Reasoning & Critical Thinking

1. For Better or Worse?
2. To Err is Human
3. And the Award Goes To...
4. Survey Says...
5. Heed These Words
6. Return to the Future
7. Be A Literary Agent

Creativity & Design

1. Play It Again
2. Sell This Setting
3. Mural Magic
4. Love That Sound!
5. Look and Listen
6. Outside the Box
7. The Jig is Up

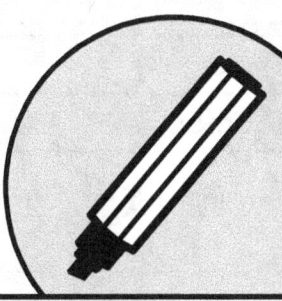

OTM18131   ISBN: 9781770788565
© On The Mark Press

_____ 's Personal Reading Record

Try to read material from a variety of genres. Record your information on the chart. Use this key to tell the genre of your book.

Title:	Date:
Author	Genre:

Title:	Date:
Author	Genre:

Title:	Date:
Author	Genre:

Title:	Date:
Author	Genre:

Title:	Date:
Author	Genre:

Title:	Date:
Author	Genre:

Title:	Date:
Author	Genre:

Title:	Date:
Author	Genre:

Title:	Date:
Author	Genre:

Looking back at your Reading Record, what is your favorite genre?

_____

OTM18131   ISBN: 9781770788565
© On The Mark Press

Book Report Activities Tracking Sheet

Name: _____

Color the box of each completed activity.

Vocabulary Development

- ☐ 1. It's About Time
- ☐ 2. Sentence Sense
- ☐ 3. Similes and Metaphors
- ☐ 4. Stick to the Basics
- ☐ 5. Creating a Glossary
- ☐ 6. In My Words
- ☐ 7. In My Mind I See …

Identifying Important Information

- ☐ 1. Historically Speaking
- ☐ 2. Reference Round Up
- ☐ 3. Story Tree
- ☐ 4. What's Cooking?
- ☐ 5. The Mystery News
- ☐ 6. Mythology Facts
- ☐ 7. Pictures Matter

Character Analysis

- ☐ 1. Fantastic Characters
- ☐ 2. Out of This World
- ☐ 3. A Room of My Own
- ☐ 4. This Song is Dedicated to…
- ☐ 5. Just Between Us
- ☐ 6. In Honour Of …
- ☐ 7. The Good, The Bad, The In-Betweens

Summarizing & Sequencing Events

- ☐ 1. Cartoon Caper
- ☐ 2. Prose to Script
- ☐ 3. Story Chain
- ☐ 4. It's All About Time
- ☐ 5. Take a Peek
- ☐ 6. And Then What happened?
- ☐ 7. Get in the Game

Reasoning & Critical Thinking

- ☐ 1. For Better or Worse?
- ☐ 2. To Err is Human
- ☐ 3. And the Award Goes To…
- ☐ 4. Survey Says …
- ☐ 5. Heed These Words
- ☐ 6. Return to the Future
- ☐ 7. Be a Literary Agent

Creativity & Design

- ☐ 1. Play It Again
- ☐ 2. Sell This Setting
- ☐ 3. Mural Magic
- ☐ 4. Love That Sound
- ☐ 5. Look and Listen
- ☐ 6. Outside the Box
- ☐ 7. The Jig is Up

OTM18131 ISBN: 9781770788565
© On The Mark Press

IMPORTANCE OF VOCABULARY DEVELOPMENT

Intermediate students can competently apply word skills and strategies to derive meaning from words. Generally, they can effectively use a dictionary and thesaurus. They require both oral and written opportunities to experiment further with more difficult vocabulary and figurative language.

This section will include:

- A review of prior skills and knowledge.
- An introduction to new terms and ideas: making a glossary, paraphrasing, and identifying examples of imagery.

Students may require a formal lesson for some skills before attempting the response activity.

ACTIVITIES & SKILLS COVERED IN THIS SECTION

Activity #	Name of Activity	Skill Focus
1	It's About Time	Identifying temporal words and phrases
2	Sentence Sense	Types of sentences and their functions
3	Similes & Metaphors	Identifying and explaining similes and metaphors
4	Stick to the Basics	Identifying nouns, adjectives, verbs, and adverbs
5	Creating a Glossary	Identifying key words and creating a glossary
6	In My Words	Paraphrasing
7	In My Mind I See ...	Identifying and explaining examples of imagery

MODELING A BOOK REPORT ACTIVITY

Mini Lesson for **"In My Words."**

- Give the students a copy of a paragraph whose content may have more than one interpretation.
- Discuss and decide on a definition for "paraphrase."
- Record the definition on chart paper to assist students while doing the activity.
- Instruct the students to rewrite the paragraph, sentence by sentence, in their own words.

- Ask students to read their answers. Discuss any differences in interpretation.
- Ask students if the paragraph's meaning was clearer once it was rewritten in their own words.
- Give students a copy of the worksheet **"In My Words"** to use with their own books.

OTM18131   ISBN: 9781770788565
© On The Mark Press

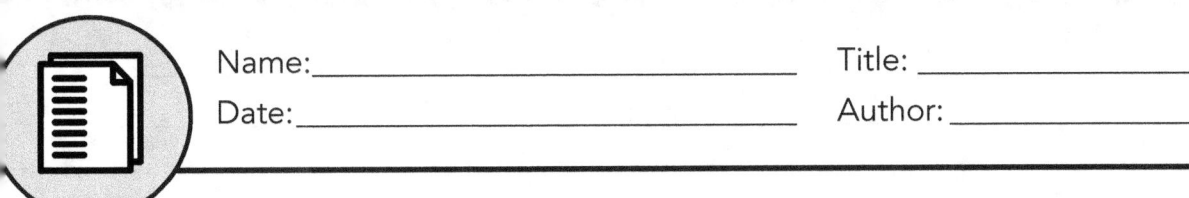

Name:_____ Title: _____

Date:_____ Author: _____

It's About Time

Temporal words and **phrases** help us to understand the passing of time in a story.

> **Examples:** later, soon, after, throughout the night, by the next morning, when he became a man

Events in a story take place over a period of time. The author will guide you through that time by using temporal words and phrases.

Beginning with Chapter 1, look for words and phrases that the author uses to show the passing of time. Find at least 20 examples of temporal words and phrases in your book. Record your answers on the chart. Tell the number of the chapter where you found your examples.

	Examples of Temporal Words and Phrases	Chapter #
1		
2		
3		
4		
5		
6		
7		
8		
9		
10		
11		
12		
13		
14		
15		
16		
17		
18		
19		
20		

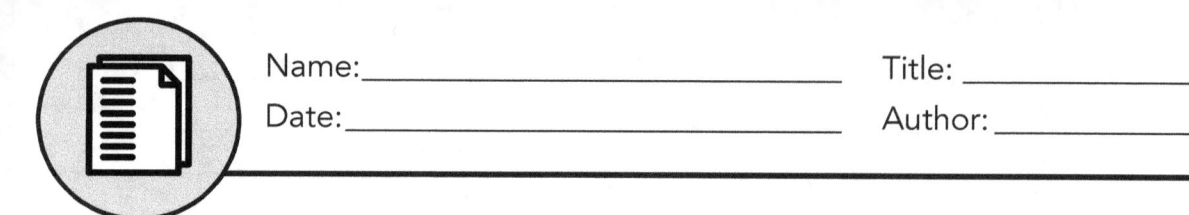

Sentence Sense

Good authors use a variety of sentences when writing a story. Each type of sentence has a different purpose and punctuation.

- An **assertive** sentence states a fact.
- An **imperative** sentence gives a command.
- An **interrogative** sentence asks a question.
- An **exclamatory** sentence expresses strong emotion.

Choose a section of your story to look for different kinds of sentences. Find **three** examples of each type of sentence. Record your answers on the chart.

Assertive Sentences: state facts	Page #
1. _____	_____
2. _____	_____
3. _____	_____

Imperative Sentences: give commands	Page #
1. _____	_____
2. _____	_____
3. _____	_____

Interrogative Sentences: ask questions	Page #
1. _____	_____
2. _____	_____
3. _____	_____

Exclamatory Sentences: express strong emotion	Page #
1. _____	_____
2. _____	_____
3. _____	_____

OTM18131   ISBN: 9781770788565
© On The Mark Press

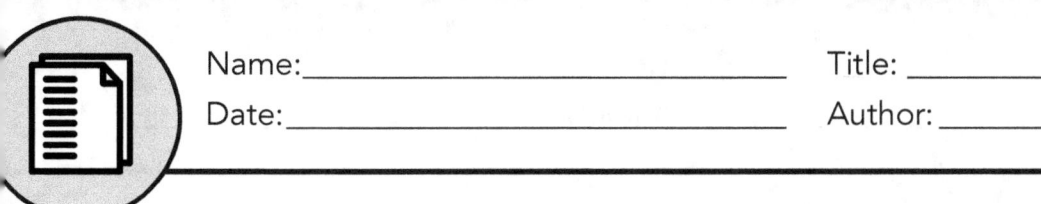

Similes and Metaphors

When authors want to make comparisons, they often use **similes** or **metaphors**.

A **simile** is a comparison between two things that do not seem to be connected. Similes begin with *like, as,* or *seems*.

> "He crept along like a wolf on the prowl."

A **metaphor** is a comparison that uses no connecting words. Readers have to make the comparison on their own.

> "A river of chocolate syrup flowed over my ice cream."

Often we have to put our own meaning on similes and metaphors. Look in your story for some examples of similes and metaphors. Write your examples on the chart. Tell if the example is a simile or metaphor. Write **S** or **M**. Write your meaning for the expression.

Expression from story	S or M	My meaning for this expression

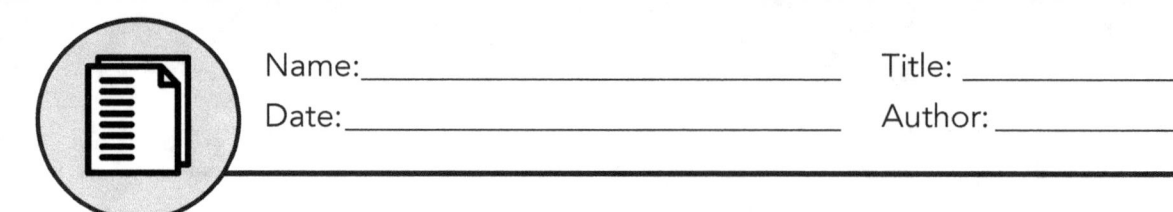

Name:_____ Title: _____

Date:_____ Author: _____

Stick to the Basics

Good authors use appealing basic vocabulary: nouns, adjectives, verbs and adverbs.

Choose a section of your story to find proof of good basic words. Write your answers on the chart below. Find six examples for each part of speech. Record the page number where you found each example.

Nouns: name a person, place or thing	Page #
1. _____	_____
2. _____	_____
3. _____	_____
4. _____	_____
5. _____	_____
6. _____	_____

Adjectives: describe nouns	Page #
1. _____	_____
2. _____	_____
3. _____	_____
4. _____	_____
5. _____	_____
6. _____	_____

Verbs: action words, "doing"	Page #
1. _____	_____
2. _____	_____
3. _____	_____
4. _____	_____
5. _____	_____
6. _____	_____

Adverbs: describe the action	Page #
1. _____	_____
2. _____	_____
3. _____	_____
4. _____	_____
5. _____	_____
6. _____	_____

Recognize nouns, verbs, adjectives, adverbs

OTM18131   ISBN: 9781770788565
© On The Mark Press

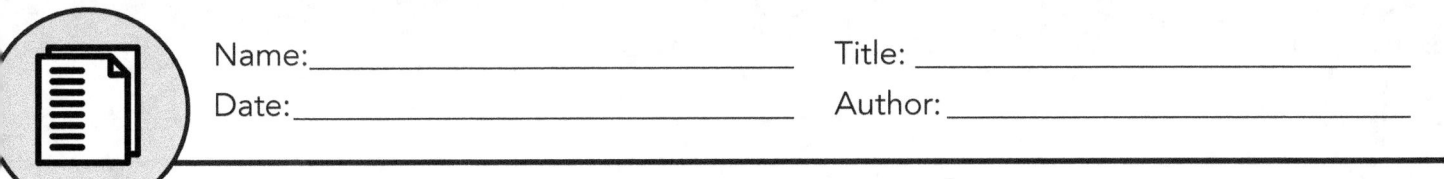

Name:_____   Title: _____

Date:_____   Author: _____

Creating a Glossary

In this activity, you will be creating a glossary for a non-fiction book.

> **Examples:** science, history, geography, sports, technology, arts, cooking

Tell the type of non-fiction book you have chosen: _____

A **glossary** is a list of **difficult words** and their **meanings.**

- A glossary explains the meanings of unusual words
- Words are in alphabetical order
- Most books have their glossary at the end of the text.
- Many glossaries will list the page where the word is found.

Find **ten difficult words** in your book and make a glossary of them. Remember to put the words in **alphabetical order.** Record your answers on the chart.

Word	Meaning	Page where word is found

OTM18131   ISBN: 9781770788565
© On The Mark Press

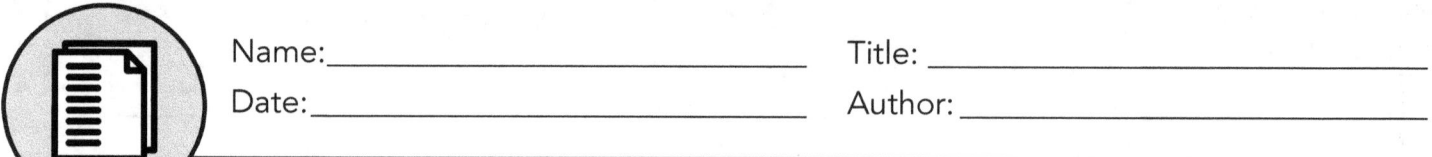

Name:_____   Title: _____

Date:_____   Author: _____

In My Words

We may not always be clear as to exactly what an author is saying. Sometimes, we may have to think about a passage in our own words in order to understand the intended message.

To **paraphrase** is to **restate** the thought of a passage in more **simple** and **clear language**. **Paraphrasing** makes the message more understandable.

A good paraphrase must:

- be clear and easy to understand
- contain all the ideas of the original passage
- not contain any ideas that were not in the original

Choose a short paragraph from your story that you found unclear. Copy the paragraph onto the lines below.

_____

_____

_____

_____

_____

_____

_____

_____

Rewrite the paragraph in your own words so that the message is clearer.

_____

_____

_____

_____

_____

_____

_____

_____

_____

_____

OTM18131   ISBN: 9781770788565
© On The Mark Press

Name:_____ Title: _____

Date:_____ Author: _____

In My Mind I See ...

Imagery refers to words or phrases that help us to imagine what someone or something is like.

Imagery helps readers to form a **mental picture** of sights, sounds, smells, tastes and feelings. Settings, character descriptions and stories about nature have many examples of imagery.

Skim over your story to find one or two paragraphs that you think are very descriptive. Copy the paragraph(s) onto the lines below.

_____

_____

_____

_____

_____

_____

_____

_____

Use a highliter to mark the descriptive parts of the paragraph.

Write examples of imagery from your highlited notes. Tell what sense or feeling they appeal to.

Example of Imagery	Sense or feeling they appeal to

IMPORTANCE OF IDENTIFYING IMPORTANT INFORMATION

Students in Grades 7 and 8 have refined their comprehension skills and are usually competent in identifying and stating important information. The next step is to extend this skill to more complex topics. Oral practice with this skill should precede written activities.

This section will include:

- A review of prior skills and knowledge.
- An introduction to new skills: awareness of types of reference books and their features, interpreting information in mythology.

Students may require a formal lesson for some skills before attempting the response activity.

ACTIVITIES AND SKILLS COVERED IN THIS SECTION

Activity #	Name of Activity	Skill Focus
1	Historically Speaking	Identifying important settings and locations
2	Reference Round Up	Identifying types of reference books and their uses
3	Story Tree	Identifying facts about characters, events
4	What's Cooking?	Facts about characters, plots, setting, mood, theme
5	The Mystery News	5 W's of a mystery; illustrate
6	Mythology Facts	Identifying facts about gods and goddesses
7	Pictures Matter	Clarifying information by illustrating facts

MODELING A BOOK REPORT ACTIVITY

Mini Lesson for **"Story Tree."**

- Give the students a copy of a short story that can be used to focus on the basic literary elements of characters, setting and plot.

- Read the story. Ask students to think mainly about these three elements.

- Give students a copy of the worksheet **"Story Tree"** to use with the shared reading selection.

- Have students highlite words in the passage that can be used for each numbered part of the Story Tree.

- Discuss answers. Complete worksheet using shared ideas.

- Give students a copy of the worksheet **"Story Tree"** to use with their own books.

OTM18131   ISBN: 9781770788565
© On The Mark Press

Name:_____ Title: _____

Date:_____ Author: _____

Historically Speaking

In this activity you will be creating a map to show important locations and events.

In **historical fiction**, the places may be real or imaginary. In **factual history** accounts, you will need to make sure your illustrations are accurate. Check an atlas if you need help.

Before printing was invented, maps had to be drawn by hand and then colored and labelled. You can make your map look old by following these steps:

Step 1: Preparing the paper

1. Use a piece of white paper 12" x 18" (30 cm x 46 cm).

2. Crumple the paper into a ball, being careful not to tear it.

3. Unfold and flatten your paper.

4. Using a paintbrush, cover the paper with a wash of strong cold tea.

5. Let the paper dry. Blot some parts with a tissue if you want to make some parts look faded.

Step 2: Preparing your idea

1. Review your book to select the most important locations and events.

2. Make some jot notes about the places you plan to include.

3. On a separate sheet of paper, make a draft copy of what your map will look like.

Step 3: Your good copy of your map

1. Remember your map will need a title, a compass point and a legend (depending on your story).

2. Transfer the ideas on your draft copy to your "old" paper.

3. Add color whenever you can.

4. Label important places or make small information boxes if you are explaining something.

5. You may wish to mount your map on a background of colored construction paper.

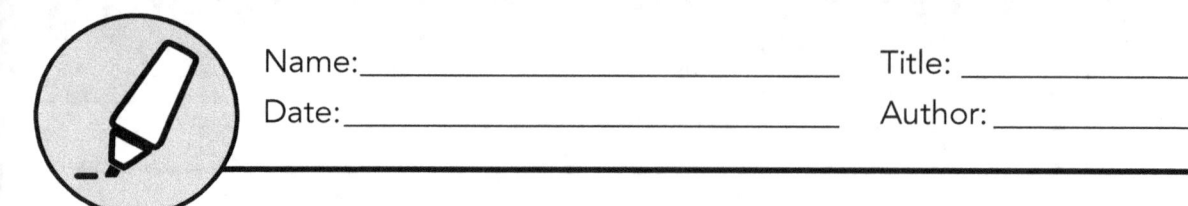
Reference Round Up

Reference Books are useful when writing reports or for looking up facts. Commonly used reference books are:

- **Almanac:** published once a year; contains calendars, dates, facts about the weather and government history; statistics on population, industry and farm products.

- **Atlas:** a book of maps that contains facts and figures about places. Information includes charts, maps, tables; locations of cities, towns, roads; relationships of land and water.

- **Dictionary:** contains the words of a language arranged alphabetically. Usually it tells their syllabication, pronunciation, definition and word origin.

- **Encyclopedia:** includes information on topics in every field of knowledge. It is concerned with the *who, what, when, where* and *how* as they relate to facts about people, places, events and things.

Think about the book you have just read. Consider ideas or words that you would like to know more about. Select one example from your book that would require using each of these reference books. Write your examples on the chart.

Reference book that I would use to learn more about words and ideas in my book	Example of words, phrases or ideas from my book
Example: Altlas	I have just read a fiction book about Irish immigrants and their dangerous voyages to come to North America to settle. I would like to trace their path from start to finish.
Almanac	
Atlas	
Dictionary	
Encyclopedia	

Use a variety of reference materials

OTM18131   ISBN: 9781770788565
© On The Mark Press

Story Tree

Create a Story Tree using information about the characters, plot and setting.

Follow this plan:

1. Name of the main character.

2. Two adjective to describe the main character

3. Three words that describe the setting: where the action takes place.

4. Four words that tell what the main character wanted.

5. Five words that tell what happened to almost prevent the main character from getting what she or he wanted.

6. Six words telling how the main character finally got what they wanted.

7. Seven words that describe your favorite part of the book.

8. Eight words telling why you would recommend this book to a friend.

1. _____

2. _____ ,

_____

3. _____ ,

_____, _____

4. _____ ,

_____ ,

_____ , _____

5. _____ ,

_____ , _____

_____ ,

6. _____ , _____ ,

_____ , _____ , _____

7. _____ , _____ ,

_____ , _____ ,

_____ , _____ , _____

8. _____ , _____ ,

_____ , _____ ,

_____ , _____ ,

_____ , _____ ,

What's Cooking?

In cooking, a recipe lists all the ingredients to mix together. It also gives some direction on how to mix those ingredients.

These are the ingredients to include in your recipe.

- **Setting:** tell where the story takes place
- **Plot:** tell what happens in the story
- **Characters:** tell the names of the main characters and if they are good, bad, funny, etc.
- **Mood:** tell if the story is happy, silly, sad, scary, serious
- **Theme:** tell the message of the story

Recipe for: (title of book) _____

Begin with (setting) _____

_____

Add one plot where _____

_____

_____

_____

Mix in (characters) _____

_____

_____

Sprinkle with: (mood) _____

_____

_____

At the end you will know: (theme) _____

_____

_____

_____

OTM18131   ISBN: 9781770788565
© On The Mark Press

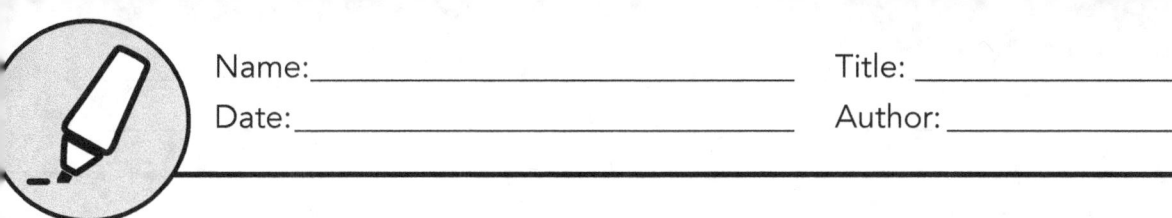

Name:_____   Title: _____

Date:_____   Author: _____

Mystery News

Imagine that you are the star reporter for The Mystery News, a newspaper that reports on mystery and adventure books.

Give a brief account of the story telling WHO, WHERE, WHEN and WHAT happens. Do not tell how the story ends. Write your account so that it will catch the interest of your readers. Illustrate an exciting part of this mystery.

_____

_____

_____

_____

_____

_____

_____

_____

_____

_____

_____

_____

_____

_____

_____

_____

_____

_____

_____

_____

_____

_____

_____

_____

_____

_____

Mythology Facts

Myths are stories that deal with characters that lived before people were on earth. These gods and goddesses often had superior powers which they may use for good or evil. Myths try to explain events or situations in life.

Tell about the gods or goddesses in your book.

Name of the god or goddess: _____

God/Goddess of: _____

Some facts about this god/goddess: _____

_____

_____

_____

_____

_____

Illustrate a part from your book that shows a god or goddess performing some deed.

Name:_____   Title: _____

Date:_____   Author: _____

Pictures Matter

How do illustrations in a book help to tell the story? _____

_____

_____

Find one example of an illustration in your book. Tell whether or not it is effective in helping you to understand the story. Support your answer.

Illustration page: _____

_____

_____

_____

Find one example in your book where you feel there should have been an illustration. Describe that section. Then do an illustration for that part.

_____

_____

_____

_____

_____

CHARACTER ANALYSIS

Intermediate students are most capable of describing and identifying with the characters in a book. To extend this skill, they need to look more closely at the characters: predict their actions; infer how those actions will impact upon the story; how characters may change throughout a story. Oral practice with this skill of character analysis should precede written activities.

This section will include:

- A review of prior skills and knowledge
- An introduction to new skills: fantasy and science fiction characters, writing a ballad, protagonists/antagonists/minor characters

Students may require a formal lesson for some skills before attempting the response activity.

ACTIVITIES & SKILLS COVERED IN THIS SECTION

Activity #	Name of Activity	Skill Focus
1	Fantastic Characters	Evaluation of a fantasy character
2	Out of This World	Attributes of science fiction character
3	A Room of My Own	Character preferences
4	This Song is Dedicated To ...	Express character information
5	Just Between Us	Compare and contrast character traits
6	In Honor Of ...	Recognize traits of heroes/heroines
7	The Good, The Bad, The In-Between	Protagonist, antagonist, minor characters

Modeling a Book Report Activity

Mini Lesson for **"This Song is Dedicated to ..."**

- Discuss the features of ballad. Sing (or read aloud) a ballad about a famous person such as Davy Crockett.
- Provide a selection of a short story with an interesting character.
- Give students a copy of the worksheet **"This Song is Dedicated to..."** to use with the selection. Provide assistance getting started. Discuss answers.

- Discuss and list some examples of simple songs that could be used for their ballads. Remember there are two parts: verse and refrain.
- Give students a copy of the worksheet **"This Song is Dedicated to ..."** to use with their individual books.

Teacher Tip: This activity might be more successful if students had the choice of working in pairs or groups of three. However, some students may prefer to work alone.

OTM18131   ISBN: 9781770788565
© On The Mark Press

Name:_____   Title: _____

Date:_____   Author: _____

Fantastic Characters

Characters that live in the world of fantasy may possess magical powers or they may own a special enchanted object that they can use at will. Just as with other characters, they often must rely on their own thinking and wits to deal with their problems. Often, they are on a mission to learn how to use their special powers or objects wisely.

What special magical power does the main character possess? Describe it.

_____

_____

_____

Does the main character own a special enchanted object? Explain.

_____

_____

_____

Describe a situation where the main character used their power. Tell where and when the situation took place and what happened to the characters involved.

_____

_____

_____

_____

Did the main character use their powers wisely? Support your answer.

_____

_____

_____

_____

Name:_____ Title: _____

Date:_____ Author: _____

Out of This World

Science Fiction characters live in a bold and speculative world. In their futuristic situations, they face man-made and other world challenges. While they are facing these challenges, they often experience the same doubts, fears and dreams as we, the readers, do.

As these characters explore new worlds, they may meet new species in their travels. They are most likely to befriend those creatures that share their hopes, fears, and dreams.

Think about a part of the story where the main character met a member of a new species.

What was his/her first reaction to this new creature? Why do you think they behaved in this way?

_____

_____

_____

_____

As the story progresses, how does the main character treat this new creature? What could be some reasons for the main character's behavior?

_____

_____

_____

_____

_____

At the end of the story, how would you describe the relationship between the main character and the creature? Describe any changes that the main character has undergone in his/her beliefs.

_____

_____

_____

_____

_____

_____

OTM18131   ISBN: 9781770788565
© On The Mark Press

Name:_____   Title: _____

Date:_____   Author: _____

A Room of My Own

Whether characters live in a log cabin, a space station, a splendid castle or a two bedroom apartment, they probably have a private place to call their own.

Think about your own private space. What things are in your surroundings that help to create a peaceful spot where you can think, dream or just have time alone? List some of those things in your private space.

_____

_____

Think about creating a special room for your main character that could be their private space.

- What colors would brighten the walls?
- What are the character's interests or hobbies?
- What special items or furniture might be found in this room?

Illustrate this special room in the space below.

_____ 's Room

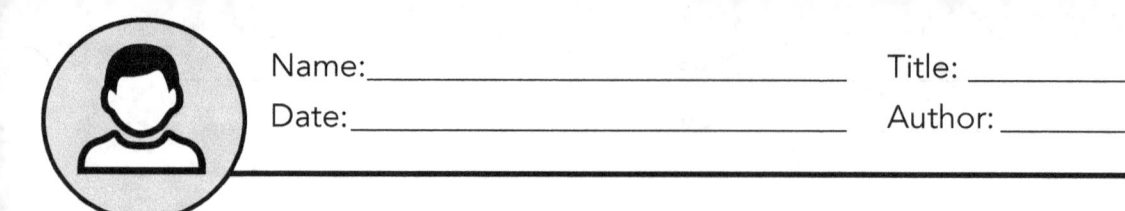

This Song is Dedicated to ...

Many ballads have been written about real or legendary famous people. These ballads contain information about the person's life and accomplishments.

Usually a ballad:

- Is written in rhyme

- Has verses that contain information about the person

- Has a refrain that is repeated between verses. The refrain usually contains the person's name and one or two facts about that person.

Write a short ballad consisting of 2-3 verses and a refrain about the main character in your book.

Before you begin to write, think of a familiar tune to use for your ballad. Make some jot notes about your character to use in the verses.

_____

_____

_____

_____

_____

_____

_____

_____

_____

_____

_____

_____

_____

OTM18131   ISBN: 9781770788565
© On The Mark Press

Name:_____ Title: _____

Date:_____ Author: _____

Just Between Us

Many readers are interested in story characters that resemble themselves. Other readers enjoy the chance to learn about characters whose personality and life is very different from their own. Either way, we get to know characters by comparing and contrasting them to ourselves.

Choose one character from your story to compare and contrast to yourself. **Compare** yourself to this character by completing the Venn diagram. **Summarize** traits about yourself and this character in the outside circle. **Record** the traits that you share in the overlapping section of the circle.

Include: personality, beliefs, actions, physical traits, personal history (i.e. only child, where you live, favorite things)

The character I have chosen is _____

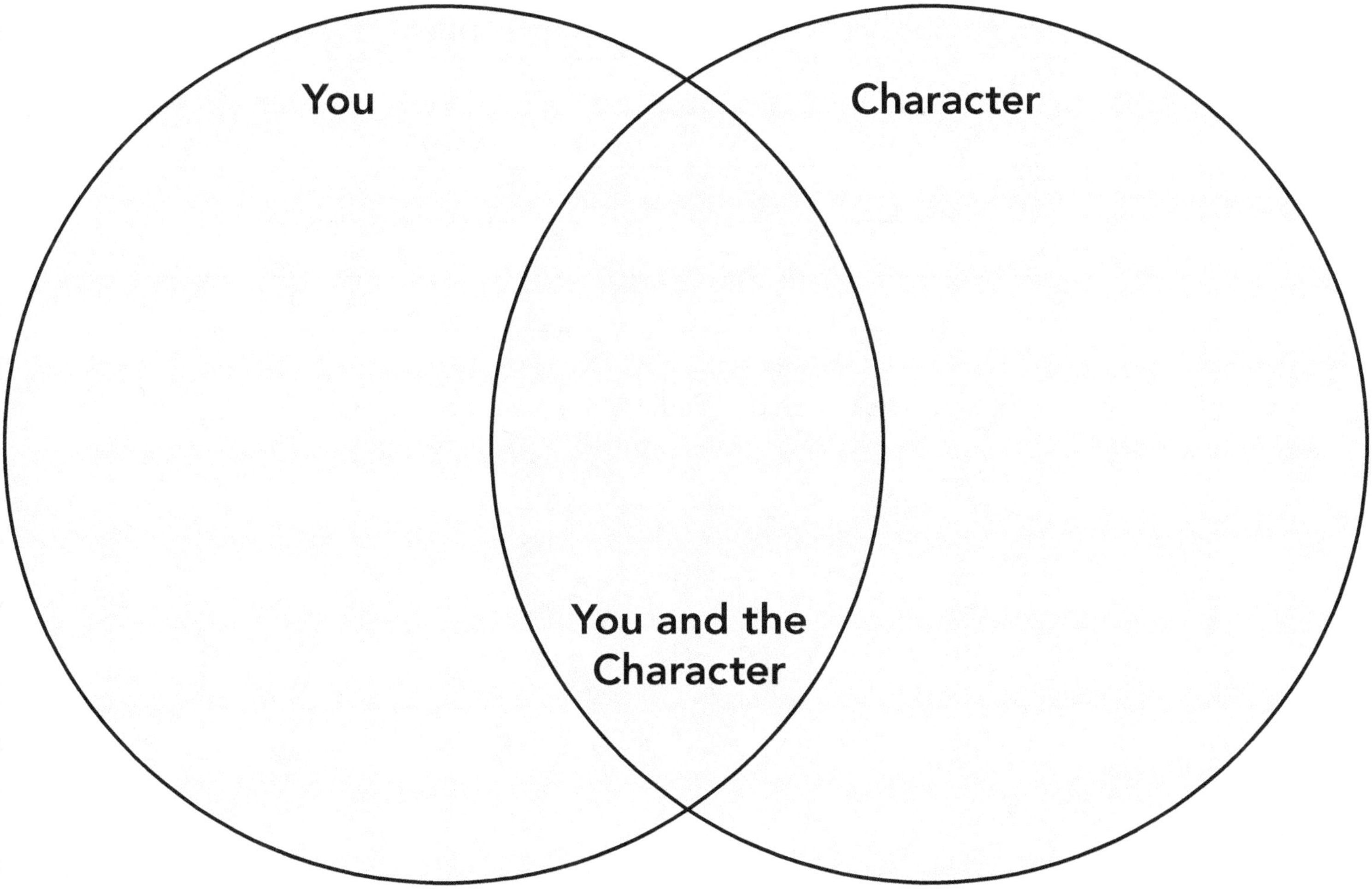

You

Character

You and the Character

Name:_____ Title: _____

Date:_____ Author: _____

In Honor Of ...

True heroes are the people who place the needs and wellbeing of others ahead of their own interests. Many story characters perform heroic acts but their efforts may go unnoticed or unrewarded.

Think of a character in your story that performed an unselfish or courageous act. Plan an award ceremony for this character to recognize their good deed. Complete the sections below to form the ceremony.

Introduction: Introduce the character by telling some facts about him/her.

_____

_____

Presentation: Describe the character's actions and how it affected other characters.

_____

_____

_____

_____

_____

_____

Design an award for your character. It can be a certificate, a medal, or a trophy.

OTM18131   ISBN: 9781770788565
© On The Mark Press

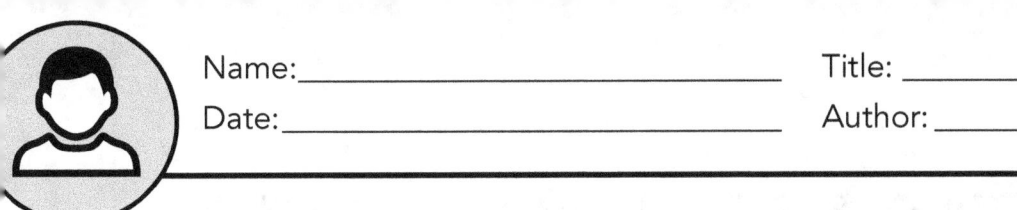

The Good, The Bad, The In-Between

Most fiction stories have three types of characters: good, bad and minor characters.

A **protagonist** is the main character who plays a major part in the development of the story. He or she will be the leader whom we regard as the **hero** or **heroine.** The protagonist may champion some cause, rescue someone or bring a villain to justice.

The **antagonist** is the character who opposes the protagonist and causes problems. While the antagonist is an important part of the story, we regard him/her as a **villain.** The antagonist is often defeated by the protagonist's thinking and actions.

Minor characters are all the other characters in the story. They serve a purpose but often appear very little in the story plot. They are the **In-Betweens.**

1. Who is the **protagonist** in your story? Give reasons for your choice.

_____

_____

_____

_____

2. Who is the **antagonist** in your story? Give reasons for your choice.

_____

_____

_____

_____

3. Who are the **in-betweens** in your story? Could some of these characters have been omitted from the story? Support your answer with your reasons.

_____

_____

_____

_____

_____

SUMMARIZING & SEQUENCING EVENTS

Intermediate students are quite sophisticated in their retelling of stories. To further extend their skills, they need written practice in summarizing and sequencing with a focus on going beyond just retelling the story. Oral practice should precede written activities.

This section will include:

- A review of prior skills and knowledge
- An introduction to new skills: converting a chapter into a play, creating a game board

Students may require a formal lesson for some skills before attempting the response activity.

ACTIVITIES & SKILLS COVERED IN THIS SECTION

Activity #	Name of Activity	Skill Focus
1	Cartoon Caper	Retelling a story using carton illustrations
2	Prose to Script	Converting a chapter into a play
3	Story Chain	Using events to retell a story
4	It's All About Time	Historical fiction: illustrated timeline
5	Take a Peek	Sequencing steps to provide a preview
6	And Then What Happened?	Sequel to important events
7	Get in the Game	Create a game board using important events

MODELING A BOOK REPORT ACTIVITY

Mini Lesson for **"Prose to Script."**

- Together read a simple short story with the class. One with sufficient dialogue to convert to conversation is best.

- Co-operatively make a list of the main characters. Discuss actions and personalities of these characters. Record ideas for student use.

- In the story, highlite actual dialogue spoken by the characters.

- Model format used to create a play. Co-operatively create one version of a play for this story.

- Assign roles and have students perform their play.

- Give students a copy of the worksheet **"Prose to Script"** to use with their individual books.

OTM18131 ISBN: 9781770788565
© On The Mark Press

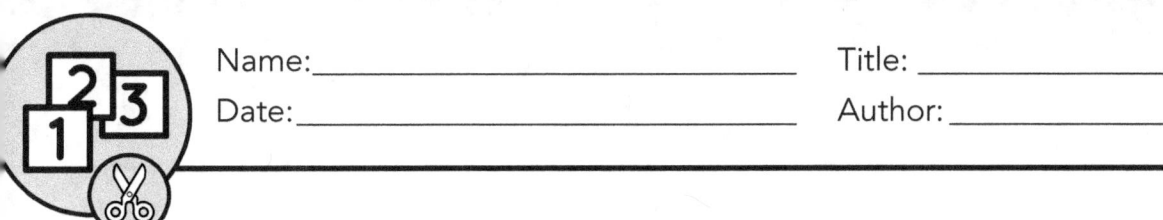

Name:_____ Title: _____

Date:_____ Author: _____

Cartoon Caper

Think about the sequence of events in your story. Choose eight events that you consider to be most important. Write a short jot note about each one. Be sure they are in correct order.

1. _____   5. _____

2 _____   6. _____

3. _____   7. _____

4. _____   8. _____

Create a cartoon version as a summary of your book by illustrating the eight events you have chosen. Use speech bubbles if the characters are speaking. Write one descriptive sentence for each frame of your summary

1	2	3	4
5	6	7	8

Prose to Script

Think about the events in each chapter of your story. Choose the chapter that you consider is the most exciting or has the most action. Write a play that tells about the events in that chapter. Follow this plan to help you.

1. List all of the **characters** in that chapter. Write a short note about each one. Include a narrator.

_____

_____

_____

_____

_____

2. **Stage directions:** tell what the characters should be doing while talking. Include these directions in your play.

3. **Narration:** try to use as little narration as possible. Rely on the words and actions of the characters to tell the story. Use conversation to give information.

4. Use props, costumes or other visual aids to add to your performance.

_____

_____

_____

_____

_____

_____

_____

_____

_____

_____

5. **Rehearse the scenes:** Ask some of your classmates if they will help you to perform your play for the rest of the class. Rehearse the dialogue and actions. Good Luck!

OTM18131   ISBN: 9781770788565
© On The Mark Press

Name:_____   Title: _____

Date:_____   Author: _____

Story Chain

Think about the main events and high points in your book. **Create** a story chain for your story that consists of at least ten links. **Summarize** each event in one good sentence.

Name:_____ Title: _____

Date:_____ Author: _____

It's All About Time

Historical fiction and **non-fiction history texts** give us a great deal of interesting information about our past. Most books in this genre portray facts over a period of time.

Make an illustrated timeline for your book. Choose at least six time events to show.

Use text and illustrations to explain key ideas

OTM18131 ISBN: 9781770788565
© On The Mark Press

Take a Peek!

Create a **preview** of your book by completing the following form.

What to Do:

1. Complete the information and the illustration.
2. Fold the bottom third of the paper **up** along the dotted line.
3. Fold the top third **down** along the dotted line.
4. On the outside of the top third, write "Take a Peek". Draw a design or illustrate an event.

Take a Peek!

Your name: _____

Title of the book: _____

Author: _____

Number of pages: _____

Genre: _____

Write five good sentences that tell what happens in this story.

1. _____

2. _____

3. _____

4. _____

5. _____

Illustrate your favorite event from the list above.

And Then What Happened?

Summarize your story by using this framework.

At the beginning of this story … _____

_____

Not long after … _____

_____

_____

Next … _____

_____

_____

Finally … _____

_____

_____

At the end … _____

_____

_____

_____

Did this story end the way you thought it would? Explain your answer.

_____

_____

_____

_____

What do you predict might happen if this book had one more chapter?

_____

_____

Summarize events
Express and support an opinion

OTM18131   ISBN: 9781770788565
© On The Mark Press

Name:_____ Title: _____

Date:_____ Author: _____

Get in the Game

In this activity you will be creating a game board using the events in your story.

You will need:

- A legal size file folder
- Index cards
- Colored pencils, markers, ruler, pencil

What to do:

- List the **positive** and **negative events** of the story. Use index cards to create a deck of **Bonus (positive)** and **Penalty (negative)** cards. Use the **Bonus** cards to move **forward** a given number of spaces and the **Penalty** cards to move **backward** a given number of spaces.
- On the surface of the open file folder, draw a winding path. Divide the path into a number of spaces. Number the spaces from the START to the FINISH.
- Around the edges of the path, draw examples of different settings from the story.
- Try to find story-related items to use as game pieces.
- Give your game a story-related name.
- Write out the game rules so your classmates can play the game.

HAVE FUN!

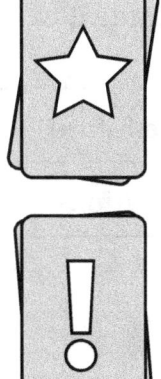

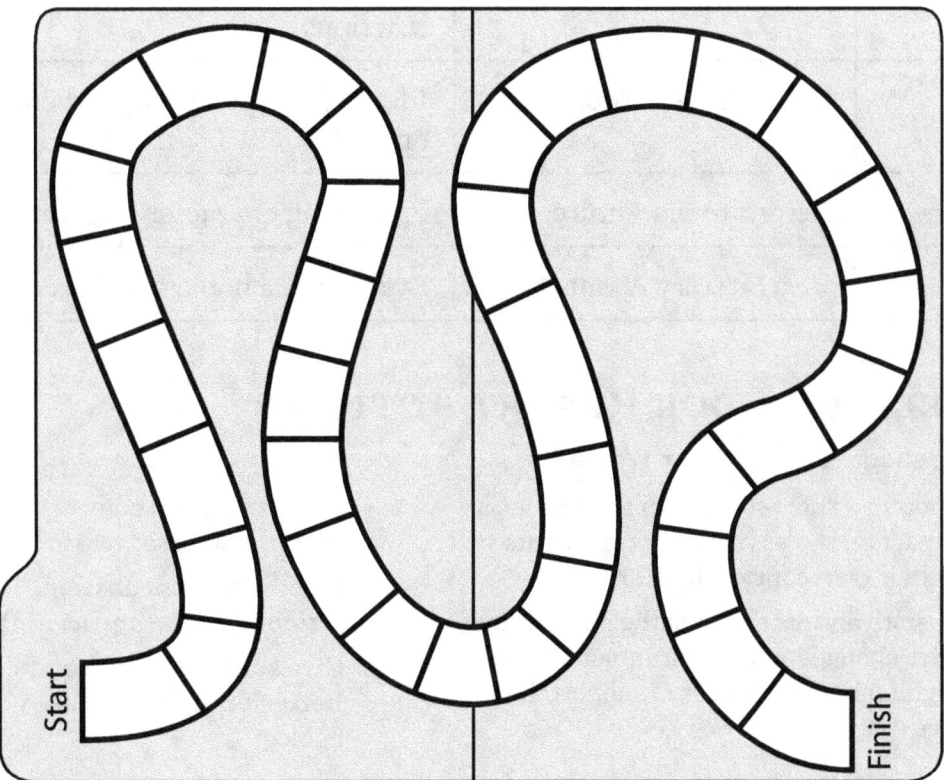

REASONING & CRITICAL THINKING

Intermediate students are increasingly more competent in the area of critical thinking skills and will be able to employ more challenging skills such as inference, analysis, and evaluation.

Oral practice should precede written activities.

This section will include:

- A review of prior skills and knowledge.
- An introduction to new skills: inferring characters' preferences, identifying the theme.

Students may require a formal lesson for some skills before attempting the response activity.

ACTIVITIES & SKILLS COVERED IN THIS SECTION

Activity #	Name of Activity	Skill Focus
1	For Better or Worse?	Impact of characters' actions on their environment
2	To Err is Human	Identifying conflict and characters' mistakes
3	And the Award Goes To ...	Evaluating a book and creating an award
4	Survey Says...	Inferring characters' preferences from their reactions
5	Heed These Words	Identifying the message/theme; relating it to oneself
6	Return to the Future	Predicting character reactions to the future
7	Be a Literary Agent	Evaluating a book; make recommendations

MODELING A BOOK REPORT ACTIVITY

Mini Lesson for **"For Better or Worse."**

- Read aloud a short story with an emphasis on impact on the environment. Students will need their own copy of the story.
- Co-operatively make a list of the positive and negative changes to the environment. Identify (by highlighting) sentences to support the choices.

- Give students a copy of the worksheet "For Better or Worse" to use with this story.
- Discuss student answers. Focus on characters' actions and the impact of those actions.
- Give students a copy of the worksheet **"For Better or Worse"** to use with their individual books.

OTM18131 ISBN: 9781770788565
© On The Mark Press

Name:_____ Title: _____

Date:_____ Author: _____

For Better or Worse?

In many stories, there is some type of interaction between the characters and their environment.

Think about the characters in your story. What evidence is there to show that the people protected or destroyed their environment?

Write a paragraph to explain the positive or negative impact that the actions of these characters had on their environment.

_____

_____

_____

_____

_____

_____

_____

_____

Draw a before and after scene to show any changes in their environment.

Before

After

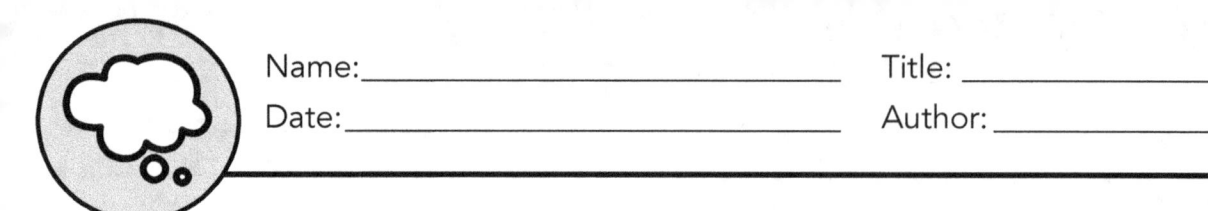

Name: _____   Title: _____

Date: _____   Author: _____

To Err is Human

Many stories contain some kind of conflict that the characters have to deal with.

Conflict can be **external** or **internal. External conflict** can be: person vs. person, person vs. nature, person vs. society (against the accepted laws, rules and standards). **Internal conflict** is the person vs. self. The character is torn in two or more directions.

Think about the conflict in your story. Write a paragraph to outline the nature of this conflict. Tell if it is external or internal conflict.

_____

_____

_____

_____

_____

_____

_____

_____

_____

What mistakes did the character make while dealing with this conflict? What do you think they learned from these mistakes? Write a paragraph to support your ideas.

_____

_____

_____

_____

_____

_____

_____

_____

_____

_____

OTM18131   ISBN: 9781770788565
© On The Mark Press

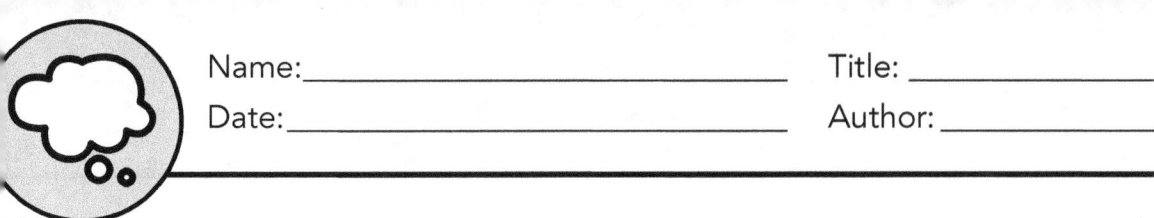

Name:_____   Title: _____

Date:_____   Author: _____

And the Award Goes To ...

Pretend that you are a member of the Outstanding Book Awards club. One of your jobs is to recognize outstanding stories.

Make up a **nomination speech** for your book. Include:

- Title of book
- Author's name and some information about this person
- Category or genre
- Features that you feel are outstanding: story line, conflict resolution, exceptional characters, descriptive language
- Why this book appeals to readers
- Any other reasons you feel that qualify this book for the award.

_____

_____

_____

_____

_____

_____

_____

_____

_____

_____

_____

_____

_____

_____

_____

_____

_____

_____

_____

_____

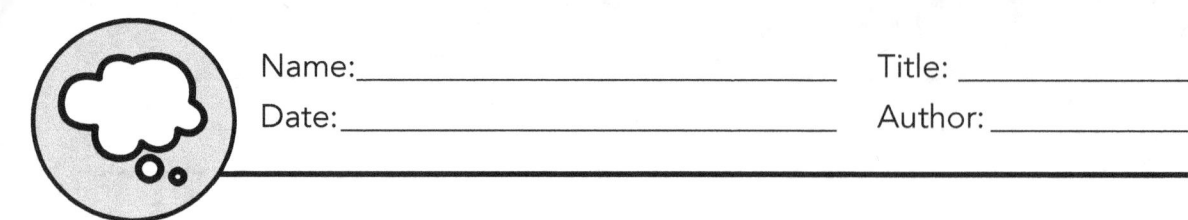

Name:_____ Title: _____

Date:_____ Author: _____

Survey Says ...

Think about your **favorite** place. What makes you so happy when you are there? Now think about your **least favorite** place. What makes it different from other places?

The main character in your book has favorite places too. You can learn about these favorite places through conversation, description or by making inferences from the character's actions and reactions.

Compile a list of ten places the character visited during the story. Beside each place, write a short description of the way you think the character felt in that place.

Place	Description of the way the character felt while in that place

Rewrite your list of places, putting the character's favorite place as #1 and the least favorite as #10. Include the short description that you wrote for each place.

#	Place	Description of how the character felt while in that place
1		
2		
3		
4		
5		
6		
7		
8		
9		
10		

How does the character's mood change as you move down the list?

_____

OTM18131   ISBN: 9781770788565
© On The Mark Press

Name: _____   Title: _____

Date: _____   Author: _____

Heed These Words

An author will try to communicate a **message** to you through the story. The **message** is the **underlying, deeper meaning** of the story.

What do you consider to be the message of this story?

_____

How does this message show you some ways that you can treat yourself and others?

_____

_____

Think about how this information might help you to live a better life.

Use the chart below to list some aspects of your life that you would like to change. Then describe how the message of this story could help you to achieve these changes.

Message in this story: _____

_____

What I would like to change about myself	How the message in the story might help
1. _____	1. _____
_____	_____
_____	_____
_____	_____
_____	_____
2. _____	2. _____
_____	_____
_____	_____
_____	_____
_____	_____
3. _____	3. _____
_____	_____
_____	_____
_____	_____
_____	_____

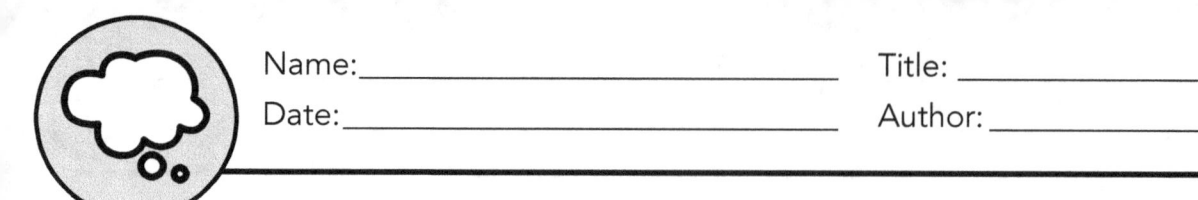

Name:_____   Title: _____

Date:_____   Author: _____

Return to the Future

Pretend that you are one of the characters in your story that has "come back" to the present 25 years after the story has ended.

What are some changes that you might see? Write a story to describe those changes. Include ideas such as:

- Different clothing styles
- Unusual food and treats (fast food, candy, drinks)
- New types of transportation

- Changes in schools and homes
- New forms of entertainment
- Any other ideas of your own

_____

_____

_____

_____

_____

_____

_____

_____

_____

_____

_____

_____

_____

_____

_____

_____

Write an informative text.

OTM18131   ISBN: 9781770788565
© On The Mark Press

Name:_____ Title:_____

Date:_____ Author:_____

Be a Literary Agent

Pretend that you are a literary agent representing the author of your book.

Write a letter to Larry Lovett, editor of young adult fiction at Super Duper Books, Inc. Explain why you feel that he should publish your book. Include:

- A description of the characters, setting, and plot
- Your opinion as to why this book would appeal to young readers
- Your prediction as to the success of this book
- Your own ideas that could help to "sell" this book

ATTENTION: Mr. Larry Lovett, editor, Super Duper Books

Dear Mr. Lovett _____

_____

_____

_____

_____

_____

_____

_____

_____

_____

_____

_____

_____

_____

_____

_____

_____

_____

CREATIVITY & DESIGN

Regardless of grade level, all students benefit from the opportunity to express their ideas in an arts form: through music, drama or visual product. Using their impressions of a story, students will create a variety of materials and performances to portray their ideas. Oral practice should precede written activities.

This section will include:

- A review of prior skills and knowledge
- An introduction to new skills: create a talking display , a jigsaw puzzle, creating a soundtrack

Students may require a formal lesson for some skills before attempting the response activity.

ACTIVITIES & SKILLS COVERED IN THIS SECTION

Activity #	Name of Activity	Skill Focus
1	Play It Again	Create a inside cover using main ideas from text
2	Sell This Setting	Create a poster designed to "sell" a setting
3	Mural Magic	Create a mini mural to retell the story
4	Love That Sound!	Select song/music for a soundtrack
5	Look and Listen	Create a talking display
6	Travel Outside the Box	Summarize story through illustrations and words
7	The Jig is Up	Create a jigsaw puzzle

MODELING A BOOK REPORT ACTIVITY

Mini Lesson for **"Sell This Setting."**

- Give the students a short story to read that has numerous descriptive settings.
- Read aloud. Instruct students to listen for descriptive parts.
- Have students highlite examples of good descriptions.

- Discuss and share students' answers.
- Ask students to choose one setting to illustrate.
- Give students a copy of the worksheet **"Sell This Setting"** to use with this story.
- Give students a copy of the worksheet **"Sell This Setting"** to use with their individual books.

OTM18131   ISBN: 9781770788565

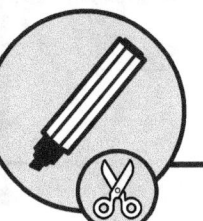

Name:_____   Title: _____

Date:_____   Author: _____

Play It Again!

Imagine that your book has been recorded onto a CD.

Design a cover for the inside of a CD case.

- An empty CD case. A transparent plastic one works best.
- White piece of paper
- Pencil, ruler, colored pencils, markers

What to Do:

- Measure and cut the piece of white paper so that it will fit inside the CD case.
- Fold the paper in half. See the example below.
- On Side 1, write a short description of the book.
- On Side 2, illustrate a scene from the story. Write the book title at the top of your picture.
- Place the strip of paper into the case. Check to be sure that the illustration and description are showing out.
- Share your "Best Seller" with your classmates.

Side 1	**Side 2**
Write your description here	Draw you picture here

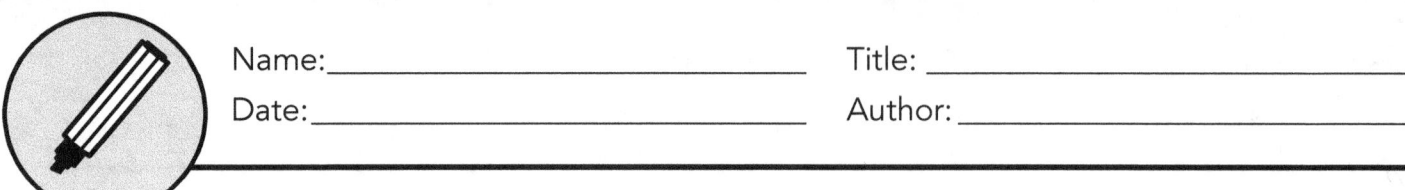

Sell That Setting

Pretend you are a real estate agent who has been given the task of selling one of the settings in your book. You need to make a poster to advertise the setting.

Select one setting from your book that you think would be easy to describe and sell. Make some notes about the things you want to put on the poster.

_____

_____

_____

Illustrate the setting using your notes and the text. Remember to use brightly colored pictures. Write a brief description under the picture.

Setting for Sale

_____

_____

_____

OTM18131   ISBN: 9781770788565
© On The Mark Press

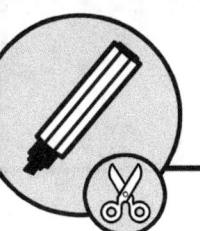

Name:_____   Title: _____

Date:_____   Author: _____

Mural Magic

In this activity, you will be retelling the story through illustrations on a mini mural.

- White paper 12" x 18" (30 cm x 46 cm)
- Pencil, ruler, colored pencils, markers
- Scraps of colored paper, yarn, ribbon, cotton balls

What to Do:

- Select the four major events from your story. Record them below.
  1. beginning of the story _____
  2. middle of the story _____
  3. high point (climax) of the story _____
  4. the ending of the story _____

- Divide the paper into four sections by drawing diagonal lines.
- Starting at the top section, number the spaces 1 to 4
- Write the title at the top of your mural.
- Starting with space #1, illustrate each of the events you have chosen. Use materials (yarn, cotton balls, etc.) if you wish to create a 3D effect.
- You may wish to mount your mural on colored paper when you have finished.

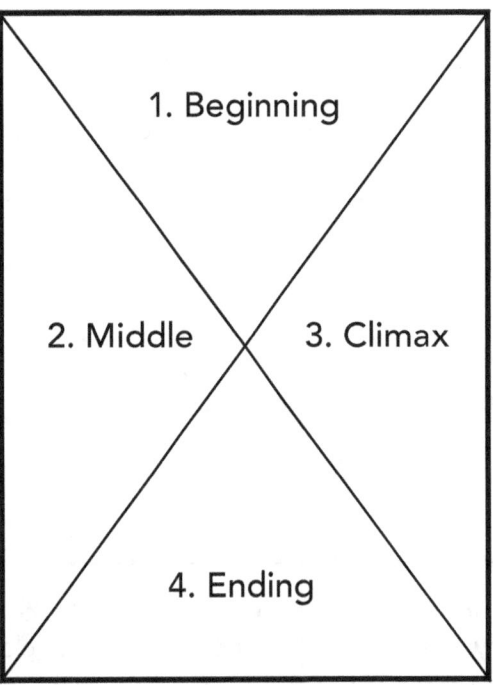

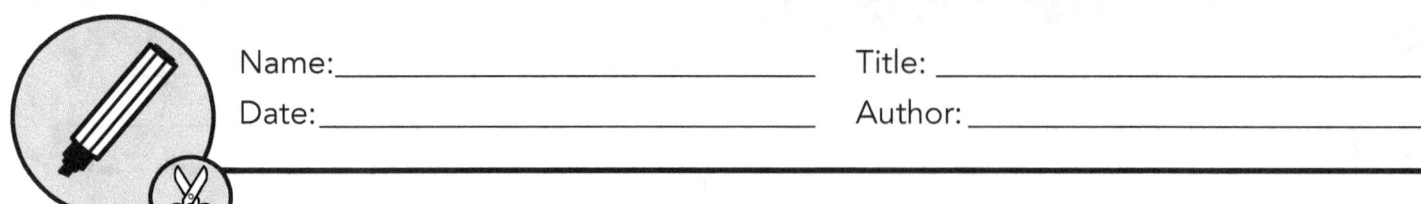

Love That Sound!

Think about the book you have just read. If the story were to be made into a movie, what kind of music do you think would be used in the soundtrack?

Select your favorite chapter. What types of emotions are caused by the events in the story?

_____

_____

Search through CDs and other music recordings for appropriate songs or instrumental music that could be used to create a soundtrack for your chapter. List the songs and music you have chosen. Give reason for your choices.

Music choice	Reason for this choice

Record your selections of music in the order that corresponds to the events happening in the story. Present your soundtrack to your classmates. Read the chapter aloud while the musical soundtrack plays in the background.

OTM18131   ISBN: 9781770788565
© On The Mark Press

Name:_____   Title: _____

Date:_____   Author: _____

Look and Listen

In this activity, you will be making a "talking display" to represent your book.

You will need:

- White paper 12" x 18" (30 cm x 46 cm)
- Pencil, ruler, colored pencils, markers
- Equipment to record and play a selection from your book.

What to Do:

- Tape a dialogue or description of an event, scene or character from your book.

- On the white paper, illustrate the section from your story that corresponds to your recorded information.

- Display your "talking display" where your classmates can listen to the recording and view your poster.

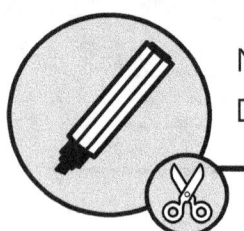

Name:_____ Title: _____

Date:_____ Author: _____

Outside the Box

In this activity, you will be creating a 3D summary of your story.

You will need:

- Cereal box (empty)
- Newspaper
- White paper
- Tape, scissors, pencil, ruler, colored pencils, markers

What to Do:

- Stuff newspaper into the empty cereal box to make it firm and solid.
- Tape the end to hold in newspaper.
- Wrap the cereal box with white paper. (just as you would wrap a present)
- On the front of the box, write the title and author's name. Illustrate the title as closely as possible.
- On the back of the box, write a short summary of the story. Illustrate some part of the story in the room you have left.
- Add catchy phrases about the book all over the rest of the book. These phrases should be interesting so other people will want to read your book.

OTM18131   ISBN: 9781770788565
© On The Mark Press

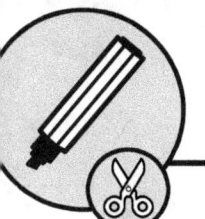

Name:_____ Title: _____

Date:_____ Author: _____

The Jig is Up!

In this activity, you will be making a jigsaw puzzle for your book.

You will need:

- Lightweight cardboard. (Bristol Board or Tagboard) 8 ½ " x 11" (14 cm x 28 cm)
- Pencil, ruler, colored pencils, markers
- Scissors
- Big envelope or plastic Ziploc bag to use to store your puzzle.

What to do:

- Write the title and author on your paper. Choose an interesting place for them.
- Illustrate a scene or event from your book. Use bright colors as much as possible.
- When you have finished your illustration, turn over the page. Using curved lines, draw spaces to represent puzzle pieces.
- Cut out the puzzle pieces. Assemble your puzzle.
- Store your puzzle in a big envelope or in a Ziploc bag. If you are using an envelope, print the title of the book and the author's name on the outside.
- Give your puzzle to a classmate to solve.